Angelus
E'Nocturnus
The Angel Babies

Angelus E'Nocturnus

The Angel Babies

CLIVE ALANDO TAYLOR

authorHOUSE®

AuthorHouse™ UK
1663 Liberty Drive
Bloomington, IN 47403 USA
www.authorhouse.co.uk
Phone: 0800.197.4150

Published by AuthorHouse 06/05/2017

ISBN: 978-1-5246-8204-0 (sc)
ISBN: 978-1-5246-8203-3 (e)

Print information available on the last page.

*Any people depicted in stock imagery provided by Thinkstock are models,
and such images are being used for illustrative purposes only.
Certain stock imagery © Thinkstock.*

This book is printed on acid-free paper.

Angelus Domini

Angelus E'Nocturnus

I N S P I R I T * A S P I R E * E S P R I T * I N S P I R E *

Because of the things that have first become proclaimed within the spirit, and then translated in the soul, in order for the body to then become alive and responsive or to aspire, or to be inspired, if only then for the body to become a vessel, or a catalyst, or indeed an instrument of will, with which first the living spirit that gave life to it, along with the merits and the meaning of life, and the instruction and the interpretation of life, is simply to understand that the relationship between the spirit and the soul, are also the one living embodiment with which all things are one, and become connected and interwoven by creating, or causing what we can come to call, or refer to as the essence, or the cradle, or the fabric of life, which is in itself part physical and part spirit.

And so it is, that we are all brought in being, along with this primordial and spiritual birth, and along with this the presence or the origins of the spirit, which is also the fabric and the nurturer of the soul with which the body can be formed, albeit that by human standards, this act of nature however natural, can now take place through the act of procreation or consummation, and so it is with regard to this living spirit that we are also upon our natural and physical birth, given a name and a number, inasmuch that we represent, or become identified by a color, or upon our created formation and distinction of identity, we become recognized by our individuality.

But concerning the Angels, it has always been of an interest to me how their very conception, or existence, or origin from nature and imagination, could have become formed and brought into being, as overtime I have heard several stories of how with the event of the first creation of man, that upon this event, that all the Angels were made to accept and to serve in God's creation of man, and that man was permitted to give command to these Angels in the event of his life, and the trials of his life which were to be mastered, but within this godly decree and narrative, we also see that there was all but one Angel that either disagreed or disapproved with, not only the creation of man, but also with the formation of this covenant between God and man, and that all but one Angel was Satan, who was somewhat displeased with God's creation of man, and in by doing so would not succumb or show respect or demonstrate servility or humility toward man or mankind.

As overtime it was also revealed to me, that with the creation of the Angels, that it was also much to their advantage as it was to ours, for the Angels themselves to adhere to this role and to serve in the best interest of man's endeavors upon the face of the earth, as long as man himself could demonstrate and become of a will and a nature to practice his faith with a spirit, and a soul, and a body that would become attuned to a godly or godlike nature, and in by doing so, and in by believing so, that all of his needs would be met with accordingly.

And so this perspective brings me to question my own faith and ideas about the concept and the ideology of Angels, insomuch so that I needed to address and to explore my own minds revelation, and to investigate that which I was told or at least that which I thought I knew concerning the Angels along with the juxtaposition that if Satan along with those Angels opposed to serving God's creation of man, and of those that did indeed seek to serve and to favor God's creation and to meet with the merits, and the dreams, and the aspirations of man, that could indeed cause us all to be at the mercy and the subjection of an externally influential and internal spiritual struggle or spiritual warfare, not only with ourselves, but also with our primordial and spiritual identity.

And also because of our own conceptual reasoning and comprehension beyond this event, is that we almost find ourselves astonished into believing that this idea of rights over our mortal souls or being, must have begun or started long ago, or at least long before any of us were even souls inhabiting our physical bodies here as a living presence upon the face of the earth, and such is this constructed dilemma behind our beliefs or identities, or the fact that the names, or the numbers that we have all been given, or that have at least become assigned to us, is simply because of the fact that we have all been born into the physical world.

As even I in my attempts, to try to come to terms with the very idea of how nature and creation could allow so many of us to question this reason of totality, if only for me to present to you the story of the Angel Babies, if only to understand, or to restore if your faith along with mine, back into the realms of mankind and humanity, as I have also come to reflect in my own approach and understanding of this narrative between God and Satan and the Angels, that also in recognizing that they all have the power to influence and to subject us to, as well as to direct mankind and humanity, either to our best or worst possibilities, if only then to challenge our primordial spiritual origin within the confines of our own lifestyles, and practices and beliefs, as if in our own efforts and practices that we are all each and every one of us, in subjection or at least examples and products of both good and bad influences.

Which is also why that in our spiritual nature, that we often call out to these heavenly and external Angelic forces to approach us, and to heal us, and to bless us spiritually, which is, or has to be made to become a necessity, especially when there is a humane need for us to call out for the assistance, and the welfare, and the benefit of our own souls, and our own bodies to be aided or administered too, or indeed for the proper gifts to be bestowed upon us, to empower us in such a way, that we can receive guidance and make affirmations through the proper will and conduct of a satisfactory lesson learnt albeit through this practical application and understanding, if only to attain spiritual and fruitful lives.

As it is simply by recognizing that we are, or at some point or another in our lives, have always somewhat been open, or subject to the interpretations of spiritual warfare by reason of definition, in that Satan's interpretation of creation is something somewhat of contempt, in that God should do away with, or even destroy creation, but as much as Satan can only prove to tempt, or to provoke God into this reckoning, it is only simply by inadvertently influencing the concepts, or the ideologies of man, that of which whom God has also created to be creators, that man through his trials of life could also be deemed to be seen in Satan's view, that somehow God had failed in this act of creation, and that Satan who is also just an Angel, could somehow convince God of ending creation, as Satan himself cannot, nor does not possess the power to stop or to end creation, which of course is only in the hands of the creator.

And so this brings me back to the Angels, and of those that are in favor of either serving, or saving mankind from his own end and destruction, albeit that we are caught up in a primordial spiritual fight, that we are all engaged in, or by reason of definition born into, and so it is only by our choices that we ultimately pay for our sacrifice, or believe in our rights to life, inasmuch that we are all lifted up to our greatest effort or design, if we can learn to demonstrate and to accept our humanity in a way that regards and reflects our greater desire or need, to be something more than what we choose to believe is only in the hands of God the creator or indeed a spirit in the sky.

It was very much my intention not to state the name of any particular place in the script as I thought that the telling of the story of the Angel Babies is in itself about believing in who you are, and also about facing up to your fears. The Angel Babies is also set loosely in accordance with the foretelling of the Bibles Revelations.

I thought it would be best to take this approach, as the writing of the script is also about the Who, What, Where, When, How and Why scenario that we all often deal with in our ongoing existence. It would also not be fair to myself or to anyone else who has read the Angel Babies to not acknowledge this line of questioning, for instance, who are we? What are we doing here? Where did we come from? And when will our true purpose be known? And how do we fulfil our true potential to better ourselves and others, the point of which are the statements that I am also making in the Angel Babies and about Angels in particular,

Is that if we reach far into our minds we still wonder, where did the Angels come from and what is their place in this world. I know sometimes that we all wish and pray for the miracle of life to reveal itself but the answer to this mystery truly lives within us and around us, I only hope that you will find the Angel Babies an interesting narrative and exciting story as I have had in bringing it to life, after all there could be an Angel Baby being born right now.

~*~

After these things I looked and behold a door standing open in Heaven and the first voice which I heard was like a (Trumpet!) speaking with me saying come up here and I will show you things which must take place after this.

Immediately I was in the spirit and behold a throne set in Heaven and one sat on the throne and he who sat there was like a Jasper and a Sardius Stone in appearance, And there was a Rainbow around, In appearance like an Emerald.

~*~

Time is neither here or there, it is a time in between time as it is the beginning and yet the end of time. This is a story of the Alpha and the Omega, the first and the last and yet as we enter into this revelation, we begin to witness the birth of the Angel Babies a time of heavenly conception when dying Angels gave birth to Angelic children who were born to represent the order of the new world. The names of these Angel Babies remained unknown but they carried the Seal of their fathers written on their foreheads, and in all it totalled one hundred and forty four thousand Angels and this is the story of one of them.

Angelus Domini

Eleventh Hour 1

Angelus & Nocturnus I

Angelus Nocturnus in the announcement of the Angel of the Lord declared unto him by the Holy Spirit, of whom is instructed to pour out forth upon the seventh canonical hour, after receiving unto himself the grace of his heart, that those who were kept and sustained within the final moments of the entire world of the Dome being plunged into the darkness, and in being cast from their sight in being overwhelming overcome by the Angels of the Empyreans, that through his heavenly incarnation made known by the message of the Earths renewal and transformation, that he should pass through the stillness of time, through his passion, in beginning the restorations afforded and brought back to the fullness of its glory, as prophesied by the resurrection of the revelations of life.

As Angel Nocturne steps foot upon the charred and baron land, instantly the ground becomes invigorated and fertile, except that yet, there is no Sun within the sky, but instead a shimmering blanket of tiny stars glowing like fireflies, flickering in the pitch of a blackened night, things have died before, but not all things are dead, and yet things have been born before, but not all things are alive to see, or to witness their own becoming, and yet if I whisper, cannot all things hear me, and yet if I touch all things, are not all things responsive to me, even here in the death of their sleeping and slumber, still life is waiting for a word, or a touch to set themselves free, and to send themselves forth, turning from their ceaseless motions to begin pronouncing once again the wheels of destiny and time.

Like the hand of God I shall sweep across the face of the land and take breadth and stride across the expanse of the Sea and in and upon the inner and outer regions within, much before heaven has reawakened and stretched forth her first beams and rays of light upon the face of Mankind's imagination in taking his and her first footsteps upon the places that I have redeemed yielding unto the restorations of life, and yet nothing can breathe without my whispering of it, and nothing can see it without the foretelling of my heart to open their eyes towards it, for not all things can walk within the light of my shadow, and not all sight can be restored unto the visions of their dreams whilst sleeping, for here is the place of what once was, will not be, even unto to the memory of it, for I come and yet I go in moving as a motion of time in eternity, but blink and I am gone, think and I am no more, for momentarily I am the dusk after the dawn, and yet I am left to decorate the night sky with burning flames of infinite particles of lights, burning like candles much before the beginning of wisdom had invented it for the flowers of such poetry and might.

I shall soar like the forces of a comet and in gaining momentum like an organic tide, purging and washing against the stricken Dome, soaring across the all engulfing, and the all consuming infinite blackened skies, descending upon the darkness's of Earths' stratosphere, weaving upon the dark matter of surrealist activities in conjuring and summoning forth the hypnotic embers of the emotional, and the scarred ruinous sub conscious shattered inspirations of their erotic dreams, feverishly feeding, and sowing, and drawing upon the subtle and the wildest of affections of the influential spheres of the constellations, in gathering and binding them together, from one end of the omega to the other, mindful of the astronomical chaos and desires of Capricornus through to Ophiuchus, unceasingly, and unwaveringly to ignite the blazing Sun, and to call upon the Sunset of my birth and death cries, as I pass thriftily through, to the gates and the gravity of the desecrated volume of the drudgery of the planets, from Mercury to Pluto, shall I spread the seed of the vineyard in fulfilling the cups of the thirsty Seas, and to wash and to drink from the bosom of the eruptions and tumultuous heartbeat of the magma of the agitated stirring arousement of the yawning Earth.

For now that the seasons are assembling themselves together, in rotating within the elements of the Earth, the Air, the Fire, and the Water, and of that quintessential matter that is the material, formed of the immortal æther, born of the substance that is most precious and mostly important in order to fill the regions of the above, and also that of the terrestrial sphere, as such am I destined to plant and resurrect the seeds of the indigenous vineyard within the forgotten garden, whereupon the root of the ancient Alkebulan is to be forged and erected, in becoming embedded and planted, and directly tied and unified as a fortified tree of sustenance for all of its' people's, extending itself beyond the several world's, in unifying the Earth and the Empyreans, and going forth and into and beyond the realms and the branches of the Universe, in shaping and connecting the cultures in union to with their deities, and in restoring the knowledge of the forbidden fruit, in restoring the significant sacred icons, and in the enactment and reconnection of the spirit with the soul, and the soul with the body, and the body with their places of origin throughout the rebirth of their heavenly renaissance

Angelus Domini

Eleventh Hour 2

Angelus & Nocturnus II

So as to venture through the aftermath of these once decorated and now deconstructed ruins, towards this desecrated iconoclastic aftermath, torn down and abandoned wastelands, except that this is not the beginning of the end, or the end of the beginning, but much rather a continuation of another verse, another chapter, another superior and yet unannounced word, waiting to be uttered by one's ability to formulate sounds, the whisper of sentences and spoken gestures, without encouraging the same afflictions and debilitations to take place or become infected, like sticks and stones and broken bones strewn across the expanses, but words, bold and brass words, as such superfluous and superficial words that have hurt one another besides, like a hundred thunder storms brewing inside a contemptuous heart, the weak and the lowly, the mighty and the strong, fallen like petals in the fullness of their bloom, now found to be decomposing and retreating back into the earthly bosom of natures grasp, crawling back into the sediments amongst the soils and, battered and eroding away upon the rocks, replenishing the stocks of life, ready and waiting to be forged by the earthly elements once again, formed by the nostrils instilling life into the lifeless veins, to set free the fire of ignition causing ripples in the beating of the stillness of their hearts.

And yet for the day to follow night, and for the night to follow day, then let all things knowingly born again agree we me that it must be so, for some things are born to die and yet some things are born forevermore to be brought back to life upon their incarnations, for the world was not born out of this birth, except that the world was conceived in its creation, and yet the universe was not born, except that the universe was his covenant with the created, and yet if all things living are born to die, then why are these things of this conception brought before this fulfillment, are we not always in agreement whilst we are sleeping, does nothing sleep in the midst of this covenant awaken out of the dark, or does everything conceived in this covenant, abstain from their agreement, if death and life are also in agreement with one another, then which was to come first before the beginning of wisdom, if death had defied life, then what is life if not defeated in the conception of a baseless untruth, and yet are all things to be greeted as dead, as before the hour that this universe did awaken, or was it that death was alive upon waiting for them the living to come into their inheritance, so why have the living inherited death, and where will it lead us now beyond this realm, or is it that death did not exist, except that all life was squandered and wasted away, and led us into the drudgery of a lesser existence, an unavoidable truth, and yet does not the smell of death linger within the air, is not the seventh canonical prayer spoken upon the very hour in this event, where all things are considered, and yet if there are other things to be considered such as those which are two of kind, then are not death and life two of a kind, and so where did you go when death took you, as surely you were well aware of the transition of the places that you have visited in life, and yet if death were no more, then what is the importance of this life upon its' sole purpose and duty, for surely if you do not agree with this universe, then are you not still alive and yet sleeping.

Of all things that are living, first let us make a way and a preparation for them that are arising and waking from out of the bosom of truth, for these are the things that are immeasurable, and yet within the eve of my absence, still they that are called forward, and yet forevermore shall still be found to be presiding over the simplest of noble truths, as to what needs are to be explained away, and as to what examples shall be sustained within the next phases and stages of this construction, if only for those that are found to arising out of the foundations of this unwritten history and adopted philosophies, if only to be pronounced by hierarchical of the Empyreans, and laid out before them as much as the Heavens have become laid out before us upon its declaration, and so it is upon hearing this debate, that through this instruction of sound, that the willful nature of the politika is refined and defined, until the exercising force is freed from those who have laid hold to it dearly as a sacred matrimonial deed, bound and destined for the first seeds and the fruits of those beneficiaries becoming, a new world within its infancy taking shape from the properties of its own influences, and yet upon its declaration, there are those of whom are born to be adverse to it, and yet further still, there are those who shall not abide within it, and yet even more so, there are those who shall seek to denounce it, and there are those who shall seek to overthrow it, and there are those who shall be have naught else to do with it, but as it is, it shall serve to stand, and as it is, it shall come to pass, as all shall be deemed to be a witness to it, for it is called forth from the first breath of the first branch, which is the time elect, and yet upon its journeying, it shall grow and change, and develop, and gain momentum, and evolve, and adapt, and nurture, and yield and govern and give itself over to all things, up until all of the seeds in the vineyard have grown to be fruitful in the fullness of their maturity.

For the breath of the first branch did not divide you, as much as the Earthly soil was not divided, and the Sea did not cause division of itself, as even the mountains were not set aside from you, except that the further away you are, then surely the more you can gaze upon the unchartered horizon, but what of the wonder of the sights, which did you seek to define, to then conceal, or to conquer, or to overcome, or to change, or to claim without the divination of your heavenly inheritance, surely we should have given praise and worship to the simplest of these noble truths, in accepting that this is so, as much as we are.

For were it not for the intervention, or the manipulations, or the rearrangement, or the things that were made not by your hand or mine, but by the ways and the nature of the sculptor, not by the image but by motion of the brushstroke, not by the sounds, but by the influences upon their intention, as it is only the breath of the first branch that crosses the boundaries, and yet it is only the continuity that establishes to afford these religious efforts, for the further away you are, it is the perception that perceives the limitations, which by all measurements of the imagination, which are none, as all things are first made whole by the breath which is life itself, especially concerning the cause, and the nature, and the purpose of you within this creation.

As it is upon the divinum of this the opus dei, that upon the seventh day, that such gifts and attributes are given over to you, to compliment you in your times of thirsting for the guidance of the holy spirit, for upon the evenings morrows, which are not gathered together in thy sight, but rather in thy dreaming of the horologion moments, the time of time itself, which is hidden and concealed within thyself, in knowing that my impression is only one of a forgotten memory, prepared for that of a sober awakening, if only to recall where I had once travelled and been too upon countless nights, still remaining, and yet to inform and remind you, that I have wandered through the realms of dreams in leaving no footprints and yet casting only shadows for all those of sobriety to see that the daylight is only sent to recover you, and to reinvigorate you, and to reinvent you once again, for the eye is inside the mind, and yet the mind is also inside of I, as consciousness, and yet residing beneath the surfaces of the awaiting dawn am I, made ready to appear upon the request of the setting Sun, and yet also influential upon the subtle ripples arising with the Moon.

Angelus Domini

Eleventh Hour 3

Angelus E'Nocturnus III

So as to venture through the aftermath of these once decorated and now deconstructed ruins, towards this desecrated iconoclastic aftermath, torn down and abandoned wastelands, except that this is not the beginning of the end, or the end of the beginning, but much rather a continuation of another verse, another chapter, another superior and yet unannounced word, waiting to be uttered by one's ability to formulate sounds, the whisper of sentences, and spoken gestures, without encouraging the same afflictions and debilitations, like sticks and stones and broken bones strewn across the expanses, but words, bold and brass words, such superfluous and superficial words that have hurt one another besides another, like a hundred thunder storms brewing inside a contemptuous heart, the weak and the lowly, the mighty and the strong, fallen like petals in the fullness of their bloom, now found to be decomposing and retreating back into the earthly bosom of natures grasp, crawling back into the sediments amongst the soils and eroding rocks, replenishing the stocks of life, ready and waiting to be forged by the earthly elements once again, formed by the nostrils instilling life into the lifeless veins, to set free the fire of ignition causing ripples in the beating of the stillness of their hearts.

For the day to follow nocturne's night and for the night to follow diurnal's day, then let all things knowingly born agree that it must be so, for some things are born to die and yet some things are born forevermore to be brought back to life upon their incarnations, for the world was not born, but the world was conceived in its creation, the universe was not born, except that the universe was his covenant, and yet if all things living are born to die, then why are the things of this conception brought before this fulfillment, are we not always in agreement whilst we are sleeping, does nothing sleep in the midst of this covenant, or does anything conceived in this covenant, abstain from this agreement, if death and life are in agreement with one another, then which was to come first before the beginning of wisdom, if death had defied life, then what is life, if not defeated in the conception of a baseless untruth, are all things to be greeted as dead before the universe awakens, or was it that death was alive upon waiting for them the living to come into their inheritance, so why have the living inherited death, and where will it lead us now beyond this realm, or is it that death did not exist, except that all life was squandered and wasted and led us into the drudgery of a lesser existence, an unavoidable truth, and yet does not the smell of death linger within the air, is not the seventh canonical prayer spoken upon the very hour in the event where all things are considered, and yet if there are other things to be considered such as those which are two of kind, then are not death and life two of a kind, and so where did you go when death took you, as surely you were well aware of the transition of the places that you have visited in life, and yet if death were no more, then what is the importance of this life upon this sole purpose and duty, for surely if you do not agree with this universe, then are you not still alive and yet sleeping.

Of all things that are living, first let us make a way and a preparation for them that are arising and waking from out of the bosom of truth, for these are the things that are Immeasurable, and yet the in the eve of my absence, they that are called forward shall be found to be presiding over the simplest of noble truths, as to what needs are to be explained, and as to what examples shall be sustained within the next phases and stages of this construction, if only for those that are found to arising out of the foundations of this unwritten history and adopted philosophies, if only to be pronounced by hierarchy of the Empyreans and laid out before them as much as the Heavens have become laid out before us upon its declaration, and so it is upon hearing this debate, that through the instruction of sound, that the wilful nature of the politika is refined and defined, until the exercising force is freed from those who hold on to it dearly as a sacred matrimonial deed, bound and destined for the first seeds and fruits of these beneficiaries becoming, a new world within its infancy taking shape from the properties of its own influences, and yet upon its declaration there are those of whom are born to be adverse to it, and there are those who shall not abide within it, and there are those who shall seek to denounce it, and there are those who shall seek to overthrow it, and there are those who shall be have naught to do with it, but as it is, and as it shall stand, and as it shall come to pass, all shall be deemed to be a witness to it, for it is called forth from the first breath which is the time elect, and yet upon its Journeying it shall grow, and change, and develop, and gain momentum, and evolve, and adapt, and nurture, and yield and give itself over to all, until all the seeds of the vineyard have grown to be fruitful in the fullness of their maturity.

The breath did not divide you, the Earthly soil was not divided, the Sea did not cause division of itself, the mountains were not set aside from you, except that the further away you are, then surely the more you can gaze upon the unchartered horizon, but what of the wonder of the sights did you seek to define, to then conceal, or to conquer, or to overcome, or to change, or to claim without the divination of your heavenly inheritance, surely we should have given praise and worship to the simplest of these noble truths, in accepting that this is so, as much as we are, for were it not for the intervention, or the manipulations, or the rearrangement, or the things that were made not by your hand or mine, but by the ways and the nature of the sculptor, not by the image but by motion of the brushstroke, not by the sounds, but by the influences upon their intention, as it is only the breath that crosses the boundaries, and it is only the continuity that establishes to afford the religious efforts, for the further away you are, it is the perception that perceives the limitations, which by all measurements of the imagination, are none, as all things are first made whole by the breath which is life, especially concerning the cause, and the nature, and the purpose of you within this creation.

As it is upon the divinum of this the opus dei, that upon the seventh day, that such gifts and attributes are given over to you, to compliment you in your times of thirsting for the guidance of the holy spirit, for the evenings morrows are not gathered together in thy sight, but rather in thy dreaming of the horologion moments, the time, which is hidden and concealed within thyself, in knowing that my impression is only one of a forgotten memory, prepared for that of a sober awakening, if only to recall where I have travelled and been upon countless nights, and yet to inform and remind you, that I have wandered through the realms of dreams in leaving no footprints and yet casting only shadows for all sobriety to see that the daylight is sent to recover you, and to reinvigorate you, and to reinvent you once again, for the eye is inside the mind, and yet the mind is also inside of I, conscious, and yet residing beneath the surfaces of the awaiting dawn, made ready to appear upon the request of the setting Sun and yet also upon the subtle inner influences of the Moon.

Angelus Domini

Eleventh Hour 4

Angelus & Nocturnus IV

For they only wish to know the truth, in order, so that they can hide and conceal it, and they wish to know the truth so that they can distort and bury it, and they wish to know the truth so that they can frame it by the claim in keeping it coveted, and they wish to know the truth, so that they can lie and discard it, and they wish to know the truth so that they can mislead and reinterpretate it, and yet all truths are brought forth out of the shadows for all to see, and yet all truth is exemplary upon its declaration, and yet all truth is wisdom, and yet all truth is whispered by the breath upon the breeze, and yet all truth is the reasoning for all things to be brought back into the inextinguishable covenant of the light, so why are the forbidden forces of the discriminate lie spoken or even taught or mentioned in such revelations of the indiscriminate light, and why are the dark forces in ignorance of the presences of the light, and why is the lie so profoundly ineffective upon the powers of the influential light, did they think to believe that in their overcoming, that they would not be overcome by the Angels of the Empyreans.

Through the climb of their ascension, did they not give it one thought or suggestion, that through these acts of their own will and volition, that in doubting the principals of fear, or the careless riddance of regret, or the mistaken metaphor of error and misjudgment, is thereupon the dark places whereupon the lies may be residing, hiding and presiding over their weaknesses and failures, waiting to strike upon their feet, the weak and the weary, causing them to stumble and fall ungraciously, but instead they did not turn away from the ruin in their rising of their worthless gains, and still they did not bow to break their knees upon their ascent, but instead they stood up in the mire of their own degradation, believing themselves to be just and forthright in their mighty places of monumental idolism, empty things erected upon the backs of the misinformed and faithless, cheated out of the loss of their inheritance, tricked by the deception of a false ideology, fallen by the wayside of their own pretences, as such is the descent of the reckless ways of the foolish to think and philosophize otherwise, if only but one offering of fish, and one bowl of rice, and cup of water, and one crust of manna would have been suffice enough to fill even the emptiest of swollen bellies hungering for the truth, but instead they only offered words of chaos and confusion, casting illusions upon the world, and yet still the Earth trembled but they did not hear the quaking until it was no more, up until it was too late.

As for those that are awake in the dark, are they not still trembling to see their fate, as opposed to those who are still asleep, who still know nothing of these concealments in the trepid dark, and so how are we to bury the living if they are not to be buried alive, and how shall we awaken the sleepers if they are dead to the world, for were it not for the resurrection, then none would be awake nor alive to see it, and yet in knowing it so, then are they still not of a frivolous and carefree nature, and so if the debt is not paid, then none shall be set free, for are we not the caretakers of the living breathing entity that dwells within, albeit of a separate composition, Angels amongst them, as even the air surrounding the aether, is that also not of angelic dust, cast off from the wings astriding the backs of the straight and upright, beating against the bosom of natures grasp, and yet when we set foot upon the Earth, are we not also suddenly and once more contaminated by the poisonous seeds that seep up through the cracks in the grounds, and yet as we walk across this beaten and barren terrain, does not the ground once again beneath us become refreshed and replenished, and so how does it benefit us to compromise and compensate for what we have cared for, for so long along with the compassions of the heavenly heart full of sorrows upon the empathy of other creations, for we are not the creatures of mud and dust, pulled forth from the soil by the creators hand, shaped like clay into the forms of the unseen spirit, as we are much higher above these dominions, in drawing upon our sustenance's of substance from the distant stars within our galaxy, and yet as we struggle to break these outer shells and free ourselves from this rock of ages, still we are caught up within its mire of degradation.

So let the reparations commence, and let the restorations of revival begin, and then let the rest of us go out into the furtherest reaches and corners of these regions and announce these redevelopments, and remedy the fate of these broken fixtures, and let it be known that the Earth has become wiped clean of her infected infidelities, so that the pastures may become enabled and purified and unsubdued, and let us reconcile ourselves in the hope that in our deeds and efforts that we shall not become accursed and turned to stone in our efforts and endeavors to fulfill its destined promises, for she cannot be allowed to fail or to become lost upon the cost and the miracle of other world's that have proven unworthy and out of this heavenly grasp and reach, for the Earth cannot, and must not be left to wither and die within the infinite void of the all consuming nothingness.

As it is in this age of upheaval, that we must seek to unearth the secret obscurities of the apokryphos, and uncover the hidden will of the intentions, as sanctioned by the esoteric few, in bearing reformative knowledge and divine authority, in knowing that we must exercise and dispense the versio vulgata, so that throughout the ages their commonality can be revealed and taught throughout the genesis of all the generations, for it will be beneficial throughout the vestiges of time, if we are to recall the anagignoskomena, so that upon our parting and separation, that these glorious doxologies, may be sung, as was once sung in Ephesus and Smyrna, and Pergamum and Thyatira, and Sardis, Philadelphia and Laodicea, in giving praise and worship of our reverences towards the benevolent benedictions of the one and only alpha, if only to stir up and encourage the awakening souls, through their daily struggles and duties as they seek to abide, and to learn, and to walk alongside these passages through him, for out of nothing we came out stars, knowing nothing of what would become, with only words to establish the Sun, with only the Moon to reflect our love, to look in the mirror and to see a trace, for it is only the spirit that we cannot face, and there is only an image of the shadows that we love, and there is only the presence of our God, for how can we know you and do you no wrong, and how can we love you and yet still live apart, and how can we know you, in truly knowing you, as our God.

Angelus Domini

Eleventh Hour 5

Angelus & Nocturnus V

For we must prepare for the perpendicular root of the Ophanim to become ecliptically aligned along the celestial spheres of the Earth's terrestrial equator, as the geometric relationship between the two elementary places must be re-established and kept and maintained at all times, and at all costs, and also endured in becoming durable upon our descent, as I must seek to dispatch one hundred and forty four thousand upon each of the selected four cardinal points, and also another twelve thousand of those upon each intermediate points, and a further one hundred and forty four thousand in addition, of which who shall also be subdivided up and allocated, to be dispatched equally in-between the obliquity of the four intercardinal ordinal points, if only to indicate the coming and the going of the eight principal winds, which shall serve to prove as the celestial path along each plane and point of this rotating spheroid, in allowing for us to also, to become organized along the northern and southern hemispheres, and also in maintaining our observations of the prime meridian.

For upon removing all the afflictions of the bowl judgments, is to make heavy handed toil of the light relief needed to prepare the way of disbonding the phial and rarest of vials needed to be dispensed, in order to separate away from the evilest effects of an adverse nature of the vilest corruptions, within the contrast and absences of a much higher and sustaining force of value, for we must prepare the way in denouncing and correcting those parts which have been for so long a place of merciless and living hellenistic existence, as for so long ago when the Earth was a shinning petal and garden of beauty shining like an emerald amongst the pearls within the stars, and yet for those who are with me, it shall be left to us, that we must seek to undo, what has been for so long in becoming the widespread destruction, and the desolate waste of the dried out euphrates, and the engulfing darkness and blackened skies beneath the scorching heat of the unrelenting Sun, laid bare upon the smitten rivers and desolate seas, if only in our adherence to bind up and place a healing tourniquet upon the painful sores of those tortured soul's, where once destruction had led them into their dismal and dire incarceration.

Freedoms beckon and liberty calls out from the belly of the pit, and expressions beckon, and forgiveness calls out from deep inside the depths of the abyss, and clemency beckons, and appeals call out from the guilt in their hearts in response to their wrongdoings, and yet we must unknot the guilty ties from the innocent as these graver robbers uncover and detect the richness embodied within, and yet is denied to the blessings to remove the yoke from the eye, or reprove the stain from the heart in reconciling their unions, for how else can one be set free from the other, if the weight of the scale and the length of the judgments are disproportionate, and yet one does not balance the in-between, either all are commuted and free, or none are freed from the deeds committed before the fall, and yet if all are free to roam, then how can it be made known, to both them and one and all, that if these acts are repeated as if it were before the fall, and if history is to be committed over and over again, as before the endless wars, then let us sit and stand in his chamber upon this dereliction and insight and redirect their will and sights toward another volition and vocation of deliverance, as something permittable is more valuable within these instincts of their living, for are we not also partisan in being drawn and selected as their caretakers and keepers, then let us keep a vigil and watch from this place, and serve to guide and indicate whereupon what is good and not good upon their awakening.

If the sound is one of real admission then let us listen, and if the reverberation is one of real submission then let show concession, and if the echo is one of real remorse, then let it be followed by the vindication of us all, and let it be followed by the act of benevolence by us all, and let it be followed by the faith of us all, and then let the accursed stain be blotted out and stricken from his sight, so that it is denied any foothold of permittance in following these newly transformed souls entry into any part of these newly formed regions, for if they do not yet know this maiden Earth, then surely they are still awaiting for a heaven to become, for it is upon this remission that they have all become absolved, for twice before did we stir up the sea of glass below the throne of the Ophanim, and yet now we are instructed to break the glass and to recover the souls therein upon breaking the barriers, in setting free all the many kinds of things that are alive and living therein.

As the full deployment of eight hundred and sixty four thousand from the Empyreans shall be subdivided and instructed to carry out in maintaining and fulfilling each and every aspect and detail that they have been assigned and designated towards them, for once the seal is broken, then there shall be no turning back from the interactive connectivity of the Ophanim and its immortal influences upon all the major and minor aspects of creation, for the sustainer and examiner of truth shall do all but whisper the breath of life unto all responsive creatures both great and small and in igniting and consecrating the ground beneath their feet, thereupon also shall the same act be accounted for and fulfilled, and yet if the world were a Virgin, then who else would give birth to it.

Angelus Domini

Eleventh Hour 6

Angelus E'Nocturnus VI

For he shall unmute the dawn by unlocking one popular word, iota dēmotikós, whispered by the Meroe's and the Nubia's, and the Phoenicians, and the celestial exiles of a greater wisdom and realization, as in the beginning, when the Earth was formless and empty, as even now we are acting as a witness to these matters within the engulfing darkness, which is now upon the surface of the deep, and yet still did the spirit hover above the waters, for who else can speak of these unspeakable things, and the shape of things to come, and to follow in the days ahead, and upon how many times has it been declared, that the word of he came unto me saying, which was also revealed to them again and again by him, that they too would know the shape and the destiny of the things to come and to follow in the days ahead.

For the recipient and the benefactor must acknowledged and adhere to the frequency and the higher intelligences, in order to relay and to communicate within a wider context in maintaining their own ability to converse with each other individually, which has in the past been less understood and put beyond the capabilities of a highly developed and spoken language which is indifferent and yet closely resembles human communication, even as the noises emitted produce a different pattern to those who are still asleep aside from those who are by now wide awake.

As for the reason why the rulers of the dominions, did ignore in that they did not hear the noise of their destruction when it was revealed to them across the eternity of times, but instead did seek to divide and remove themselves from the simplest teachings of the noblest of truths, and yet even as they responded to one another in an uncivilized tongue of an educated and eloquent fashion, still no one amongst them did serve to prove unto themselves otherwise, for could they not agree in seeing that they were without the cohesive support and promises of agreements suggested and made long ago, of following the pathways towards an enlightened state of tranquility and reflection, if only to avoid this unspeakable outcome, and yet still they did not choose to comprehend that together we and stand and yet divided we fall, as did everything formerly in decline begin to stumble like a rolling rock upon the erection of the Domes, now found to be the merciful amongst the merciless, choosing to follow the paths of obscuring the truth, but instead causing separation, upon the distinction of finding superior isolation and aggravated deviations of argumentative interpretations, proving to be the destructible seed and the inevitability hastening the end of creation.

For there is no debate in heaven, and there is no discourse in conclusions, there is only the knowledge's of passages, in the processes of knowing, that within this counsel which is to satisfy that it is all encompassing the whole, and that the praises be praiseworthy upon its completed perfection, for I did not make it so, and you did not make it so, and even together we did not make it so, except that it is ours to salvage through him who made it so, that all things take shape and size and gain weight and gravity by the sounds of his murmuring thunders, so how can they be distracted from it when they are placed upon and within it, for there is nothing nefarious to obstruct us, and there is nothing to denounce upon it when we are all unencumbered, either we are all right or nothing is wrong, or whichever may prove to be the greatest interpretations of this wisdom and wise conduct, for in his counseling, there is no plot to undermine the veritas of his heart, his mind, his soul, and also of all the things given in alms and prayers, nothing was denied unto them, who built this construction Etemenanki, of Nimrods abhorrent and inherent legacy, was not the soil of this inheritance worthy enough of praises, did it not yield the goodness of the Earth for the vineyards of the fruitful and divine.

When we look at the segments and the fragments of disorder and chaos, now scattered like pieces of useless rocks and stones, and if I say, if, if we are to bring us and them together, then will they also help us if we agree to help them, do you not see the endless possibilities of unity forged between the heavenly heart and the earthly body, and yet if we allow the heart and body to stray away from one another, then what shall become of us and them when the spirit of creation also abandons us and them for not maintaining these links of bonds that bound and tie all this wondrous harmony of the universe together, release your power master, as of yet in disorder and chaos we shall cling to the rock of this salvation, and yet in this salvation, is it not of the power that we speak of in saying that we must help them if we are to acquire true salvation, not for ourselves but for their sakes, for only then can we untie the tourniquet in announcing that the wounds have become healed, and so therefore, are we not all free to pursue the strength and the power of his wisdom, for he did not abandon the heavens as the Earth fell away, and so we must have faith and trust in the completeness of his creation.

Angelus Domini

Eleventh Hour 7

Angelus *E'Nocturnus* VII

Where once there were oceans and seas, now there is dereliction and dust, and where once there were mountains and rivers, now there is desolation and waste, but be mindful of the words that separate us from one another, for we must remove this obstruction and obstacle and engage in enabling the words that unify them also, so undo your wrath master and increase the wealth of the Earth, and once again give it material gain and worth, and return unto Alkebulan the fullness of its merits and glory, for do not all the many things emanate and arise from out of her origins in possessing a desirable and perfect quality.

For upon this one singular iota dēmotikós do not all things take shape and before we do, and do not all things take effect before we do, and do not all things proceed before we do, and do not all things become organized before we do, and do not all things transpire before we do, and do not all things come forth before we do, then knowingly or unknowingly, do not all things become alive and responsive upon their pronouncement as we do, and yet are we not are also reactive upon their pronouncement, as did the light awaken in the dark, as did the spirit revive even itself upon this declaration, as did the heavens itself expand upon this first breath, as did everything else take their forms naturally upon this utterance, surely beginning and ending with you.

Command me once again so that I might take up this mantle of life, in that I might proceed to lead these select few Angels of the Empyreans towards a newness of oneness, in igniting and encouraging the seeds of the Earth to flower and to rise out of her ashes, and to come into the fullness of her seasonal bloom, along with the satisfaction of fulfilling her virtuous nature, let her awaken graciously in drawing nearer to the cradle and further from the grave, and remove all blame and blemishes from her, in transferring one iota dēmotikós of your pefected consciousness unto hers, instantly before death has prevailed and consumed her, and reunite her unto the tree of life amongst the other pearls of the stars.

For this is but one fraction and one miniscule portion of what you retain in maintaining within your possession, and yet of all the stars in the universe, is she still not found to be much more valuable and much more precious and much more amazing in her modest splendor, and so therefore is she not much more of an importance before she has reached extinction and the end of calamitous finality, and so therefore is it not to be found, that upon her resuscitation, that is it not so, that the whole of the balance is restored upon her presence in being brought back to liberty within the universe.

For it is not befitting of a story, and yet it has never been told, and yet you spoke it out of the consciousness of your heart, as it is also what men chose to believe, and yet it was hard to fulfill or to come by, but still they made their efforts and preparations because of it, as they too would hope to see such glorious deeds coming out of God's hands, in being received unto theirs, and yet their skies are fulfilled, as if they had depended upon the truth of it, so tell me, if what we have, is what we once had, then are not such choices now decided upon whether we hold on or to let go if what in the past has already been laid to rest.

Angelus Domini

Eleventh Hour 8

Angelus & Nocturnus VIII

For when the Earth was youthful she thought she was strong, in giving birth to a world, except that did they not all souls still belong to you, but now that she is older, has not the world become a place in which the Earth became unknown, did she begin this journey alone from the womb of your universe destined towards the grave of a golden tomb, and yet why has she suffered for so long, and how could we let this carry on, is there no more defenses in the name of God's domain, is there any more malice's to tear her apart, for I wonder if the rain and thunder still survives in her heart, for this journey begins from the seed of creation, through a passage of unrefined knowledge, hardly believed and acceptable, loving and leaving, coming and going to and fro, surely when she spoke the truth you listened to her responses, or did you not know that she was dying for reasons still unexplained and unknown, has she not expressed enough will, in declaring that within this place, that so many souls have suffered for so long.

Don't you see, that the light must endure at all costs, but without exception, is that not what we are fearful of, don't you see the very notion, that the dark is not caring or concerned about her, No, it is the darkness that wants to prevail upon the light, despite what we might find, it is the Earth that is forever exchanged and bartered away as an excessive commodity, and yet we are the products of her lifeline, so you see that the light must prevail at all costs, in escaping the creatures of the dark, as much as things cannot be sustained in the darkness, still there are creations lurking beneath her.

If she is to go down before the cross, kneeling down upon the altar, ready to be changed and washed and cleansed by your holy spirit, baptized once again to walk through your flames, heavens above, now found to be erected, standing upon this rock, do we not call Earth her name, is not every day in coming forward a blessing, or a miracle, or a prayer, has not a savior come from out of her ashes, do they not sit inside of her temple, and wonder how you would create all this through faith, is this not the true purpose why everything happens for a reason, because of her love for him.

If we wait any longer, nothing will happen, and if we pause anymore nothing will sustain, and if we become idlesome in our behavior, then nothing will succeed, for we must serve to nurture and to empower her now or never, or she will not become healed, as surely these spiritual inclinations are born of the diversity through the thoughts of a vibrational frequency, and surely as a master upon this occurrence, you possess the ability to formulate the sounds that gives quality and meaning to these attributes, and surely therefore, the very basic and primary concern is one of understanding and an opportunity now, for the beginnings of a new era of purity, and surely her attributes are to be maintained and strengthened in her becoming directed away from this language of confusion which has become the results of chaos.

For what else has shattered the fears, is now that which has become the faith of all things, and so what is the worst thing if it had already transpired, as it is within this separation that the unspeakable sorrows have become a burden to us all, surely the bride and the groom should be considered when coupled together, for when was the last time she spoke and mentioned joy, and how long must she dwell in the absence and postponement of happiness, for what has obliterated the naturalness of these sensibilities, if not to forgive and to forget, then how else upon example is she not to be remembered, as it is only the forgotten who stir in idle behavior, storing up such memories of injustices set against themselves, and so how else are these transgressions wiped away unless we all wake up.

Angelus Domini

Eleventh Hour 9

Angelus & Nocturnus IX

If nothing before us is immune to these perpetualities, and nothing can withstand against such forces, and nothing can avoid the ferociousness, then release the same from out of the cavernous craters in the ground, and free the same from the eruptions of the mountains, and allow the same from the storms upon the wind, but gift life unto her as she is waking, and gift life unto her when she is arising as the ascendant star, and gift life unto her as she is ascending, and invigorate her as she gives the same unto all her living inhabitants.

If the first breath is without sound, then guide us like the wind through the rustling of trees, and if the first words are like a child, then inform us through your precious innocence, and if the first pronouncement is a singular vow, then influence us with your presence, otherwise we shall remain confounded and left to roam in the dark, as even now the time draws closer and closer and nearer and nearer as also does the time escape us, fleeting at every opportunity in passing us by.

Are these contextual chapters wasted away upon such words that would fulfill no deliverance, is our appeal to those of the highest decree, looked down and frowned lightly upon, as a feebly minded request, are these advocative empathies found to be a petition full of futility, or will our bargaining plea issue forth a resounding glorificamus of her sacred beauty, for in her modest and ordinary form the soul is not yet dead but simply diminished and in need of administering too in the hope of curative healing.

Or will this be the gravest fall ever now unrecorded in the annals of the Empyreans, and who save none shall bare to express to mention such unbearable things, for what became of her when nobody knows, and yet unaided she had fallen into the graveyard of the abyss, and after all the seasons had come and gone away, and still she is left to wilter and die away quietly, for there was no softness in her stillness, and there was no resounding expression to raise her from out of the harshness, the bitterness, the ugliness of this unsightly foreseen decay.

Is it the woeful sound of the whimpering amidst the crying of the injured, yelps of despair unable to raise their lowly bowed and broken spirits, or is it the moanful groans of the afflicted and the hurting pains of the gashing gaping open wound, exposed upon the gasping for breath and air to relieve and to soothe it, or is it the weaknesses of the tired and the withdrawn, crawling and creeping wearily to retire upon the hardened stone for some comfort and rest, or is it the starling echo of the past ignored, neglected in the immediacy of the present shape of things to come.

Angelus Domini

Eleventh Hour 10

Angelus E'Nocturnus X

If it is not you, if you are not the one, then who must we appeal to within the light, Angelus E' Diurnal' upon our intercessions of plea bargaining, and if you are not the consequence, then to whom shall we speak too of this expiration, and if you are not the one to cease this expulsion, then to whom shall we be directed towards the will and counsel of who shall undivide us, is God dead also, figmented away, are these words that sustain in giving life no more to be heard and lifted up and expressed freely, wherefore are the tokens of whispers that once raised the mountains and rivers and streams of consciousness unto her bosom.

Then let us also gather together and administer unto God also, and let us revive him so that he too knows also of the boundlessness of his authority over love and perhaps in his wisdom and examples, we shall see his wonders overcome us, and exalt the Earth also, for God must also soften and relent from the tirelessness of his creation, yes perhaps in taking care of God all is taken care of, and yet why did we suppose to act unsupportive in declaring otherwise, so be quickened and cause the slowness to hurry, and speedily hasten, and hence forth to show him gratitude and concern, and perhaps we will beget his mercy.

For in looking over, lest we overlook, we must seek to replenish the sources that pulsate from out of his consciousness, filling up everything outwardly and beyond, in extending and lending itself toward all living and sentient things, for now it is the darkness that will dissipate and fade away, ushering away with it the fears of our concerns, as we find following behind and beneath it, the requested invitations of the breaking dawn, along with the vision, that morning has broken through and come in the form and expression of his waking wisdom.

For what we took for granted, we did not reprove upon in our own reflections, upon the formal and proper conduct of exampling thankfulness, so be quick and hasten the hosts of heaven to draw closer unto the realms of the Ophanim, and see to it that God is accompanied in his chamber, and call upon the archangels and instruct them that God is not to be kept partioned away from the sights of his creation, and go down to Nejeru and shower them with pleasing affections of patronage and adoration, and shake up the Empyreans upon the tree of life and ready them for an examination of the highest high.

let such particles float across the spectrum, in allowing for the stars to flicker against the matter of such darkness's, let the infinity of light pierces through the void, as beams of rays break through, infinitely spreading across the cosmos, let everything with senses alive, releases and announces their energies, and perhaps the future wills speedily hastens itself to greet the present, as tomorrow becomes today, and now becomes forever, enliven the spirit and calm the soul, for she sleeps no more and yet she feeds upon the first fruits of the nectar of the tree of life, the Earth lives, yes the Earth is suckling in her modest nature, the petal is beautiful, for she flowers and steadily grows stronger with each measure of the elemental forces coursing through her.

Angelus Domini

Eleventh Hour 11

Angelus E'Nocturnus XI

Unravel the string and unknot the threads, and release the planets amongst the stars, and extend unto each one of them a branch from the tree of life, so that throughout their infinite cycles, they can find the bonds and the links that unite and tie us all together, also expand upon the uniting verses, and give them room and space to take root and flower, for the savior of the Earth must also extend such virtues towards both the brotherly and sisterly planets of this universe, for the Earth is not alone in her modest existence, but is also accompanied by other forces extended to her from beyond the cycle of the wheels that turn from one realm to the next.

Unconfuse their language momentarily, and balance the thought of the emotional spirit and the masculine and feminine aspects of the planets, restore the monumental vision and fulfillment of higher ideals through your vibrational frequency, rotate the wheel encircling the subtlety of the psychic energies that embodies the centre of all esoteric living things, bring into harmony the far and the divine distant objects that pulls and separates all of us in coming together, for the Earth is not a stranger within the company of the planets and stars, but is part of their completion within its orbit.

Even though some things in heaven may remain a mystery and so therefore cannot be explained to the ordinary, whether the hand of God is bedside such things is justly so, but still I insist on saying, that of these mysterious things, God is not one of them, except for his motion across the universe, but since the beginning of time he is forever present, so how can we excuse the fact, that through his creation we have satisfied a relationship with everything between us, no God is not a stranger from some strange unknown place yet to be discovered and uncovered, for he is forever present in every activity that commences, and yet it is only the content of such knowledge's that are unfamiliar to us, even when we see the emptiest and shallowest of things full of dust within the void, still we marvel and wonder at how simple the creator is, but is this still not exceptional, no God is not separate from everything bound upon the Earth, except that what we see is only a realization of the gradual influences of the changes laid bare before us, is this not surprising enough, are not all these mysterious things tied and knotted together.

For within the dream world, I am the wide awake hypnosis of the sleeper dreaming in the night, and late within the dusk of the evening I am Angelus E' Nocturnālis, the nightened day behind the daylight, I am the remnants of the daydreamers amusements submerged beneath the light of day, I am the voice behind the prophetic prose, I am the hidden obscurity, lingering upon the edge of darkness, I am the abiding blackened shadow, walking besides them as a lowly reassuring companion, and yet I am found to be accompanying each and every stranger upon the highways of their nightmares, I am the scurrying undetectable creature, the evidential scent of the unexposed, I am the opposing duality of the diurnal occupations, I am the secret of the muses, and the conjuring of the darkest corners, upon the breaches of the mind.

Soon enough all things will stretch forth yawning giving praise to this day of days, and soon enough I must go down and depart away to remote and distant quarters, for in the shadow of my parting I shall pass on the torch that lights and leads the way, to that of my decline, for I shall fall to slumber and become as a distant memory to my successor who shall passover and transcend over me, announcing the alarming call of the morning, and the waking of the Elventh Hour.

~*~

Angelus Domini
A Tao.House Product /Angel Babies
Angelus E'Nocturnus
INSPIRIT*ASPIRE*ESPRIT*INSPIRE
Valentine Fountain of Love Ministry
Info contact: **tao.house@live.co.uk**
Copyright: Clive Alando Taylor 2017

~*~

Printed in the United States
By Bookmasters